GAME FACE

Between the Sticks

by Rich Wallace
illustrated by Tim Heitz

Calico
An Imprint of Magic Wagon
abdopublishing.com

abdopublishing.com

Published by Magic Wagon, a division of ABDO, PO Box 398166, Minneapolis, Minnesota 55439.

Printed in the United States of America, North Mankato, Minnesota.
092015
012016

Written by Rich Wallace
Illustrated by Tim Heitz
Edited by Heidi M.D. Elston, Megan M. Gunderson & Bridget O'Brien
Designed by Laura Mitchell

Extra special thanks to our content consultant, Scott Lauinger!

Library of Congress Cataloging-in-Publication Data

Wallace, Rich, author.
Between the sticks / by Rich Wallace ; illustrated by Tim Heitz.
pages cm. -- (Game face)
Summary: When the team goalie is injured during the soccer match, seventh-grader Griffin is called on to switch positions and play goal for the remainder of the season--and the playoffs.
ISBN 978-1-62402-132-9
1. Soccer stories. 2. Soccer goalkeepers--Juvenile fiction. 3. Teamwork (Sports)--Juvenile fiction. 4. Responsibility--Juvenile fiction. 5. Self-confidence--Juvenile fiction. [1. Soccer--Fiction. 2. Teamwork (Sports)--Fiction. 3. Responsibility--Fiction. 4. Self-confidence--Fiction.] I. Heitz, Tim, illustrator. II. Title.
PZ7.W15877Bg 2016
813.54--dc23
[Fic]

2015027915

TABLE OF CONTENTS

The soccer ball rolled into my zone, with two Cyclone players in pursuit. I darted to it, nudging the ball toward the sideline and moving away with it. A Cyclone elbowed me, but I pivoted hard and faked him out. With one swift motion I booted the ball up to midfield.

"Great defense, Griffin!" called Spencer. He's our goalie. Spencer gets all the credit for our four straight shutouts. But without me as the middle defender, he'd be in trouble.

No one had scored on us all season, and it looked like we were on track for shutout number five. We're a high-scoring powerhouse, thanks to my friends Torry, Marcus, and Javon up front.

I should say, we're *usually* high scoring.

With the clock ticking down toward the end of this game, we'd managed just one goal this morning. Still, 1–0 is a win. If we could hold on. The Cyclones were applying a lot of pressure.

I'd spent most of the second half clearing the ball away or trying to force our opponents into traffic. I'd been backpedaling or running sideways constantly.

I hadn't done any wheezing yet, but I was getting tired.

Javon made a nice steal and scooted along the sideline. He's the shortest player on our team, but one of the fastest, so he raced deep into the Cyclones' end of the field before anyone caught up. He crossed the ball to Torry, who one-touched it to Marcus. Marcus's shot was on target, but the goalie made a diving save.

Then the Cyclones came again, desperate to tie it up. Their defenders were on their way up, too, so our end of the field was swarming with players.

I bounced on my feet, ready to move.

No one gets by, I told myself.

Torry and Marcus double-teamed the guy with the ball. I closed in toward the goal with our other defenders.

The ball squirted free. I raced toward it, but Ernie got there first for the Cyclones. He planted his foot and drove the ball toward the corner of the goal.

Spencer dived, stretching and reaching. He deflected the ball over the back of the goal, but then fell to the ground and howled.

"My wrist!" Spencer yelled, rolling onto his back. The referee blew his whistle and ran toward Spencer, waving for our coach to come over. "Clear away, boys," the ref said.

Ernie stepped over to me. He looked shook up.

"I didn't kick it that hard," he said.

"It happens," I replied. "You didn't hurt him on purpose." Ernie's a good guy. He's in two of my classes and we've played baseball together. "Besides, I think he hurt it when he hit the ground, not the ball."

It took a good five minutes to stabilize Spencer's wrist and get him off the field. He shook his head as he walked past our team. I heard him mumble, "Finish this thing."

"Where were we?" the referee asked, glancing around.

"The Stampeders goalie knocked it out," Ernie said.

"Right." The ref nodded. "Corner kick, Cyclones."

"How much time is left?" I asked.

The ref looked at his watch. "Forty seconds when they put the ball in play." He rolled it toward the corner.

Then the ref yelled, "We need a goalie!" He was pointing at the empty net.

We'd overlooked that little detail.

"Griffin Lane!" Coach called.

"Yeah?" I took a few steps toward him.

"Get between the sticks," he said, referring to the goalposts. "Spencer left the gloves on the ground there."

"Who, me?" I asked. "You've got to be kidding." I hadn't played goalie since third grade, and I'd promised myself I never would again. I yielded seven goals in half a game back then. Seven goals on seven shots. Not a single save. Of course, I was a lot younger then—that was four years ago.

I love playing defense; it suits me just right. I'm not fast enough for the front line, and I get exercise-induced asthma from sprinting too much. Plus, there's less pressure on D than there is in goal.

"It's just for a few seconds," Coach said, trotting onto the field again. "We'll figure out a new strategy before the next one. Don't worry, this game's almost over."

Sure it was. But these last few seconds were everything. Ernie had the ball in the corner, and his teammates were packed into our goal box. Even their goalie had come all the way up the field for this final attempt. They had nothing to lose this late in the game.

I pulled on the gloves. I should have put on the goalie shirt, too, but we weren't about to ask Spencer to try to take it off. So I told the ref I was ready. The sweat on my back turned cold.

Javon shook his fist at me. "No problem, Griffin," he said. "They won't even get a shot."

Ernie lofted a high, looping kick that seemed to hang in the air forever. I stood tense, arms spread, ready to pounce in any direction. *One save*, I thought. *One save and we win.*

Torry, Marcus, and players from both teams soared into the air, hoping to head the ball away from our goal or into it. Shoulders collided and players grunted. The ball hit the ground.

Thwack! Someone kicked it. A line drive to my left, rising quickly. I lunged. The ball skidded off my fingertips and hit the net with a whoosh.

The Cyclones yelled in triumph and fell into a massive purple heap. “Goal!” someone yelled.

Torry, Javon, and the others stared in disbelief.

I got to my knees.

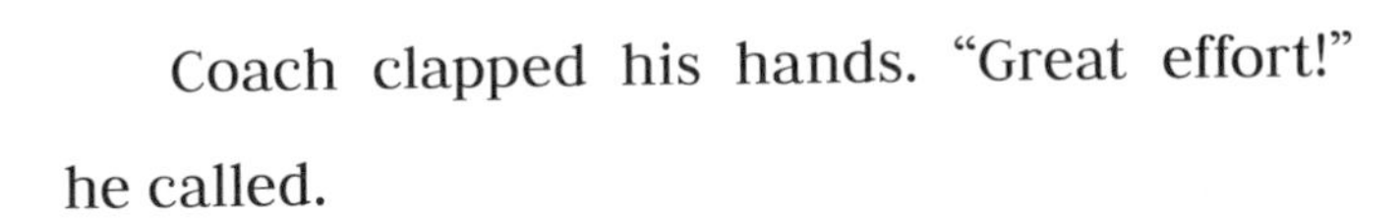

Coach clapped his hands. "Great effort!" he called.

I turned and picked up the ball. Terrible effort, I knew.

"Still time, Stampeders!" Javon yelled.

But five seconds after Torry's kickoff, the ref blew his whistle.

So much for a perfect season.

I peeled off the goalie gloves and glared at the spot where the ball found the net. First goal we'd allowed all season. First second I'd been a Stampeders goalie. Last time, too, I hoped.

I walked slowly to the bench where Coach gathered us for a postgame talk. He's fresh out of college and is very intense for a weekend YMCA coach. Every minute of every practice is go, go, go. But it's paid off so far.

"A tie doesn't hurt us," he said, running his hand through his short blond hair. "We're still at the top of the standings."

I looked at Spencer, straddling the bench with his wrist wrapped in an ice pack. His dad was with him.

"Spencer's done for the season," Coach said, nodding toward him. "We'll see what the X rays show, but it's at least a bad sprain. Obviously we'll need another goalie. Think that over, and we'll try some options at Tuesday's practice. I'm certain we'll find a good fit."

We practice twice a week, with games on Saturdays through the autumn. It's not a big-pressure league, just local kids from three or four towns. Mostly fun, except for moments like this.

"I hate losing," I muttered to Javon as we walked away from the field.

"It wasn't a loss," he said.

"It feels like one. We had it wrapped up until Coach put me in goal."

"Would have happened to any of us," Javon said. "Even Spencer. Corner kicks are tough to defend. You had no chance on that shot. None."

I let out a sigh. "Somebody better step up. Spencer was the only experienced goalie we had."

"*Was* is right," Javon said. "You've had forty seconds between the sticks now. You're practically a veteran."

"Ha!" I stopped and pulled off my shin guards. "That was the low point of my soccer career. I am definitely not goalie material. Those forty seconds should have made that clear."

"Don't be too sure," Javon said. "You actually made a nice play on the ball. Your instinct was right, but you would have needed elastic arms to reach it."

I took a long swig of water from my bottle and wiped my mouth with my hand. "I hear a sandwich calling me," I said. "It's saying 'Griffin! You're hungry. You ran your butt off this morning and you deserve food!'"

"Yeah, I hear that," Javon said. "It's saying, 'Feed Javon, too!'"

I laughed. Coach was right: a tie didn't set us back much. Next week I'd be in my regular position, passing the ball to the offense and protecting our goalie. Whoever that unfortunate person turned out to be.

TWO
Weighing the Options

I've only lived in this town for two years, and it took me a while to make friends. I've always played sports, but I was never that into them until I met Javon and he introduced me to Torry and Marcus. They're all *very* into sports, and my interest has picked up, too.

I've been on school teams with them, but I have to admit that I like these low-key YMCA leagues better. It's more ragtag—no fancy uniforms or high-pressure games against schools from other towns. Just a T-shirt and a smaller field, and only seven players at a time for each team.

Still, we play hard. I've had to use my inhaler a few times in practice, and last week I had to leave a game after running more than usual.

I ran even more than that today, but on warmer days like this I breathe easier.

My parents own the Fast Lane Café on Main Street, so Javon and I headed there. The café is only open for breakfast and lunch, but my parents are there by five o'clock every morning. So I fend for myself a lot for those meals. I like that, though, which I must get from my chef mom. I get my little brother off to school or day care, too.

We went in the back door of the café, stepping around a big crate of carrots and jars of mayonnaise. I could smell chicken soup and about a thousand other aromas. From the kitchen, I could see the dining room was very busy. My dad was talking to customers.

"Can we eat?" Javon asked me.

I nodded. "I'll make us some sandwiches. Let me check in with my parents first."

Mom was at the grill. "Hi, sweetie. How did it go?" she asked.

I'd forgotten about the game for a second. "Okay. A tie. I was the goat."

"Really?"

"He wasn't," Javon said. "We all blew it."

"A tie isn't bad," Mom said.

I winced. "This one was."

Mom flipped some chicken on the grill and pulled toasted buns out of the broiler. She can juggle more things than a circus act.

"All right if we eat?" I asked.

"Anything you want," Mom said. "Can you get it yourself?"

"Sure."

"Can you pick up Connor when you're done?" she asked. "He's been at Julie's all morning."

Our next-door neighbor looks after my little brother on weekend mornings. He's almost six, and Julie's kids are one and three, so it isn't a lot of fun for him. Sometimes I think Connor is a pain, but I know I should spend more time with him.

Javon and I sat on empty boxes in the alley behind the café and ate our chicken salad sandwiches. I outweigh him by thirty pounds, but he eats as much as I do. Maybe more. Torry and Marcus are the same way. Everything they eat burns up in about two seconds.

"Seriously, who do you think Coach will put in goal?" I asked.

"Don't look at me," Javon replied. "Any high shot would be over my head."

"Torry could do it."

"Torry can do anything," Javon said. "But we need him up front. Most of the goals we score are because of him, whether he makes the final kick or not. He sets up everything."

Javon popped his last bit of sandwich into his mouth and wiped his fingers on his yellow STAMPEDERS shirt. "You're the man, Griffin," he said, chewing. "Honest. I can't think of a better choice."

NO PARKING

"Think harder," I said. "Coach made it clear that was just for today. It was an emergency. I don't need that kind of tension."

"But goalie is not a high-pressure position on this team," Javon insisted. "Look at the scores so far. Five–zip. Three–zip twice. Five–zip again."

"Yeah, but don't forget today," I reminded him. "We ended up 1–1."

"Today was a fluke. Look, Spencer only had to stop about two shots a game so far this season. Including today."

"Yeah. Because I was on defense. Nobody got past me to take a shot."

"Good point," Javon said. "But you're still our best option."

I shook my head. "We'll see who steps up on Tuesday," I said. "But write this down: I am not a candidate."

Javon came with me to pick up Connor. My parents wouldn't be home for at least three hours.

Connor was in Julie's yard, bouncing a ball off the garage.

"Did you eat yet?" I asked him.

"Yeah. Peanut butter."

I thanked Julie and waited until we were home to ask him how his morning went.

"Boring," Connor said. "Baby stuff."

I remember what it was like when I was too little to be on my own at all. The difference was I didn't have an older brother who could step in and kill the boredom.

"Next Saturday, I'll take you to my game," I said. "Today we'll play some basketball. That's not boring, right?"

"Nope." Connor smiled.

I figured Torry and Marcus would show up soon. We hang out together most afternoons, playing sports or video games. They live across the street from each other a few blocks away from us, so they've been friends forever.

We shot baskets until they arrived. Connor's pretty athletic for six—more like my friends than like me.

Torry yelled hey as he ran up the driveway. Connor tossed him the basketball, and he made a reverse lay-up. Torry is ultracompetitive and could play sports twenty-four hours a day. Marcus is more laid-back, but he's a great athlete, too.

"Three-on-two today," I said to Torry, nodding toward Connor. "Get it?"

Torry smiled. "What teams?"

"Me, you, and Connor," I said. That meant Marcus and Torry would guard each other, and I'd face Javon. I'm about five inches taller than Javon, but he can jump. Connor could roam the court, and we'd do our best to set him up for shots.

Torry immediately drove past Marcus and streaked toward the basket. Javon darted over to stop him, and Torry flipped the ball back to Connor. He dribbled twice, then made a clean lay-up as Marcus made a big show of trying to block the shot.

"Beautiful," Torry said.

Connor beamed. He doubled-up on Marcus on defense and managed to steal the ball. Marcus winked at me. Connor dribbled toward the basket and Javon hovered over him. He bounced the ball to me and I scored.

"Great D, Javon!" Torry said. "You finally have an opponent you're taller than."

"Not by much," Javon said. It was true. Connor is tall for his age, so Javon is only an inch or so taller than Connor.

We played like that for an hour. Javon and Marcus were good at keeping things competitive so Connor wouldn't feel babied. But he made his share of baskets and laughed a lot.

"You guys trounced us," Javon said when we took a break. "I think Connor should switch to our team next time. He made all the difference."

"You weren't too bad," Connor said. "You kept it close."

Javon grinned. "Thanks," he replied.

"The next game will have to wait," Torry said.

We all stared at him. He was always up for another game of anything.

"I'm starving," he said. "I haven't eaten since breakfast."

"Why not?" Javon asked.

Torry shrugged. "I don't know. I was mad about the end of the game and didn't even think about eating until now."

I pointed toward our house. "We have leftover chicken in the fridge."

He shook his head. "My dad made me some sandwiches. I'd better go home and eat 'em. You guys can come with me. Then we can play some more hoops at my house."

"Cool!" Connor said. He jumped up and started walking down the driveway. He turned and said,

"Let's go, guys." It was great to see how happy he was to be included.

We talked about the goalie situation while Torry ate.

"Maybe we could alternate," Marcus said. "One-quarter of the game apiece."

Torry shook his head. "You need consistency back there. You'd never get comfortable like that. It has to be one guy."

That was true. I'd had no time at all to get comfortable today. Gloves on. Corner kick. Wham!

"Besides, we'd be less effective on offense," Javon said. "The three of us make a huge difference up front. It wouldn't be the same with two."

"It wouldn't be two," Marcus said. "Somebody else would move up."

"Yeah," Javon replied, "but face it—the rest of the team isn't that good."

Torry pointed at me. "Griffin."

"What?"

"What do you think?"

I ran through the roster in my mind. Our other defenders could do it—Charlie or Jameer—but then what? There are only nine players on the team, and now we're down to eight with Spencer out. That left just Ramon or Luis, and neither one looked like a goalie to me. Short like Javon, and not good jumpers like he is.

"Maybe someone will surprise us," I said.

"Right," Javon said. "Maybe Ramon will grow seven inches taller this weekend, or Luis will turn into a grizzly bear."

"I'll do it," Connor said. "If you need another player, I'll join."

"Sorry," I said, squeezing Connor's shoulder. "Too young. Next year we'll get you on a team though. In your age group."

We played another hour of basketball, but I was wiped out by then. A soccer game and two hours of basketball was more than enough for me, even though these guys would have kept going until dark. Connor, too.

"That was awesome," Connor said as we walked home. "Can we play with them every Saturday?"

"I don't see why not," I said. It had been fun. I didn't always enjoy all-out, two-on-two basketball games with the most competitive guys on the planet. We'd still have plenty of time for those, so I figured even Torry would go along with some laid-back games with Connor. Torry spends time with his little sister, and Javon gets to hang out with his older brother sometimes. So I was ready to do the same for Connor.

"I think you should play goalie," Connor said.

"Maybe," I replied. But I didn't tell him I was afraid that would happen. Like Javon said, I was looking like the best option.

And that didn't sound like fun at all.

THREE

Lineup Shuffle

It rained all day on Tuesday but started to clear just before school ended. I met Javon by our lockers.

"Think Coach will cancel?" I asked.

"Doubt it. A few puddles won't make any difference to Coach. It would take a hurricane."

I grabbed my knapsack. "I saw Spencer in algebra but didn't get to talk to him. He had his wrist wrapped up, but no cast."

"Maybe that's good news," Javon said. "If there's no cast, it isn't broken. I know where he is."

We ran down the hall and out a side door. Javon yelled to Spencer, who was waiting for his bus.

"What's the deal?" Javon asked.

"It's a grade 1 sprain," Spencer said.

"How bad is that?"

Spencer held up his wrist. "It hurts. But the doctor said I'll be fine in two or three weeks."

We had three more games. "So, you might be back for the last one?" I asked.

"Nah. I'll be ready for basketball season, but I can't risk reinjuring this."

I frowned.

Spencer smiled. "I'll yell as loud as I can for you, Mr. Goalie."

"Don't count on that," I said.

"Torry already told me it would be you."

"Who elected him coach?"

"I think everybody agrees," Spencer said.

"Everybody but me." I turned to Javon. "Come on or we'll be late." Practice was at the field behind the Y, six blocks away.

"Seen Torry and Marcus?" Javon asked.

"They're probably at the field already," I said. "Probably raced there."

We were the last to arrive, and the others were already running laps.

"Take two," Coach said, clapping his hands. I set my knapsack on the bench and started jogging. Javon sprinted off to catch the others.

We did passing drills and worked on fakes and defense for a while before Coach got down to business.

"We have a big hole in the lineup, obviously," he said. "I want everybody—all eight of you—to take a turn at goalie today."

Fair enough. But this looked like a setup. Make it appear that everyone was being considered, even though I'd be the lucky winner.

"I'll go first," I said, raising my hand. Might as well get it over with.

Coach set up two lines of players about twenty yards from the goal and put Javon on defense halfway between them and me. He rolled a ball to Torry, who charged forward, with Charlie running parallel. Javon shielded Torry, who crossed the ball to Charlie.

I stepped forward and tried to shorten the angle between Charlie and the goal. His shot bounced to my right, almost out of reach, but I managed to smack it before it crossed the line. My knee came down in a puddle.

The ball popped into the air. Torry met it with his forehead and drove it into the net.

"Not bad!" Coach said.

I shook my head. One save. One miss. I could do better than that.

Marcus was next, coming at me full steam. Again, Javon edged him away from the goal, but that left Jameer wide open in front. Marcus stepped over the ball and dodged left, then scooted it back to Jameer.

Jameer stopped the ball and unleashed a fierce kick. Right at me. I caught the ball and hugged it against my stomach.

“Yes!” I shouted. Then I shut my mouth. Too much enthusiasm might make Coach think I enjoyed this.

I made three more saves and gave up two goals. But games don’t usually unfold like a two-on-one drill. With good passing in a drill, someone is always open, leaving the goalie (me!) unprotected.

There wouldn't be so many uncontested shots in a game. So my record was pretty good.

"Torry," Coach said. "Get in there."

I handed Torry the gloves. "It's not easy," I said.

"No kidding."

I ran to the front of one of the lines. As a defender, I didn't get many chances to score, so I took advantage of my practice opportunities.

Marcus was on D now, so this was no lark. We'd have to get past him and then beat Torry, too. I

nodded to Luis, who passed me the ball. I circled wide and Marcus didn't challenge me. He stayed between me and the goal and watched Luis from the corner of his eye.

I passed back to Luis at the top of the goal box, then called for the ball again. This time I charged. Marcus took the bait. I pivoted and kept the ball out of his reach. But I had no shot.

Marcus was right on me and Torry had the side of the goal covered. Luis drifted behind me and I sent him the ball. His shot was high and curving wide, but Torry was quick enough to get to it. He scooped it up and Coach blew his whistle.

"Great work," Coach said. "It's all about the angles. When we give up a shot from the front of the goal, the goalie has too much area to cover. But on offense, that's our aim. Get the ball in front and shoot for the corner."

I scored a couple of times, managing to sneak the ball past Jameer and even Marcus. Other than

Torry, nobody really stood out as a goalie. Nobody did too badly, either.

And I have to admit, I sort of liked it this time.

We ran a couple more laps, then sat on the bench.

"What did we learn?" Coach asked.

"That playing goalie is tough," Marcus said.

Everyone laughed.

"Right," Coach said. "So whoever winds up doing it deserves a lot of support. On the field and off. If we give up a goal, it's on all of us. We win as a team or we lose that way. No goal falls on a single player."

I swallowed hard. I knew what was coming. There was no way he'd name Torry as the goalie. And I'd done better than anyone besides him.

"Are you up for it, Griffin?" Coach asked.

"I guess."

Javon and Marcus started clapping. I blushed. Jameer raised his fist and I bumped it with mine.

"Saturday's game will be hard," Coach said. "The Alligators have been close in every game, and they've only lost twice."

"Who replaces Griffin?" Marcus asked.

"Good question. Jameer will shift to the middle on defense. Ramon, Luis, and Charlie will alternate in the other two defensive spots."

That sounded a little better. Jameer's pretty good, although I was definitely the best defender on the team. So we'd be weaker in several places—middle defense, one of the outside defensive spots, and goalie. That could be a big difference. And obviously the last game had been too close for comfort.

"We'll need a lot of goals," I said. "Something tells me we'll be giving up a few."

"No problem," Torry said. "I know how to score. Just get me the ball."

That was part of the problem, too. A lot of our goals were started by a big kick from me—up to Torry or Marcus or Javon. Were Jameer and the others capable of getting the ball upfield consistently like I was?

It was simple. We were a weaker team all of a sudden. Thursday's practice would be crucial. We still had a lot to learn.

FOUR
No Help

On Saturday morning, Connor got up before dawn and kept pestering me to take him to the field. Our game wasn't until eleven thirty, but we left the house at nine o'clock and reached the Y before half time of the first game. Ours was the third game of the day, so we had a long wait.

I found a loose ball and we kicked it back and forth in a far corner. I kept my eye on the field, watching the goalies. Anything I could learn would help me.

Coach had drilled me in the basics at Thursday's practice session, so I didn't feel entirely clueless. But it was all still so new. I told Connor what I'd learned. The more I repeated it, the more likely I was to remember it.

"A goalie has to move side to side all the time," I said. I showed him how. Connor picked it up in a second, dancing in a straight line left, then right.

I'd given him my yellow Stampeders shirt to wear. It was huge on him, but he didn't care. He tucked it into his pants and pulled it as tight as he could in the front.

Coach gave me the bright green goalie shirt on Thursday. It's a lot safer for the goalie when his jersey is a different color from the other players'.

"Here's the best tip Coach gave me," I said. "No matter where the ball is on the field, imagine it's attached to a rope that reaches all the way to the center of the goal. The key is to stay on the rope line, so you're always between the ball and the goal."

"I love imaginary things!" Connor said.

"You'll love this, too," I said. "A goalie has to make himself big." I stretched out my arms and stood tall. "Cover as much of the goal as possible."

He roared like a lion and got as big as he could.

"That's it," I said. "Big and scary!"

Torry, Javon, and Marcus showed up in time for the second game, the Sharks against the Lawnmowers. The Lawnmowers scored two quick goals and dominated the action.

"That has to be the dumbest team name I ever heard," Javon said. "Lawnmowers?"

"They're good though," Torry said. "Only one loss this season, and that was a tight one, too."

"When do we play them?" I asked. I wasn't eager to go against a team that managed so many shots on goal.

"Last week of the season," Marcus said.

Torry waved his hand. "We'll think about that when the time comes," he said. "Let's take care of business this week. We could have the title wrapped up before we even get to the last game."

I watched the Lawnmowers carefully. Hadn't seen them play yet this season. They wound up with a dominating 6–0 win. They looked as good as us. Maybe better.

All the more reason to preserve our unbeaten record.

I bought Connor some popcorn and a drink at the refreshment stand and told him to stay near our bench. Then I jogged onto the field and did a few jumping jacks by the goal.

"Fire 'em at me!" I called. My teammates started bombarding me with shots.

We were very psyched, clapping between shots and jumping up and down. We'd been sharp in Thursday's practice, and I knew we were ready.

"Bring it in," Coach called. We stacked our hands in a circle, and Coach told Connor to get in there, too.

Spencer led the chant, since he wouldn't be doing much else: "Three, two, one, Stampeders!"

We ran onto the field, and I got tested almost immediately.

The Alligators came racing down the field, making crisp passes. I kept that rope idea in mind, eyes on the ball every second. But a player broke past Jameer with the ball and zeroed in on me. He gave it one tap too many, and the ball got away from him.

I darted to it and rolled to the ground, scooping up the ball a split second before he would have

shot. He jumped over me. Close. But I had the ball, and I booted it up toward Torry.

Coach and Spencer and Connor all yelled my name. That was a nice play.

Beat 'em to the ball. That was the key.

Javon got off a shot at the other end, but the goalie deflected it and the Alligators charged again. They were quick. Their tall wing faked past Luis and ate up a lot of ground. He made a smooth pass that trickled past Jameer, and that same guy who jumped over me sprinted toward it.

Beat him there, I thought. But I misjudged his speed. He reached the ball first, dodged slightly, and fired the ball past me into the net.

It was the first time we'd been behind all season.

Javon clapped. "Get it right back," he said. "Let's go!"

I kicked at the ground. Rookie mistake. But one goal wouldn't slow us down.

Two might.

I barely had time to think before the Alligators were back in the goal box, yelling for a pass from the wing. Jameer was on the guy with the ball, but the Alligators were in my face. Charlie and Luis were totally outmanned.

Two quick passes, another hard shot into the net. We were two goals behind before Connor finished eating his popcorn.

"Help out!" I hollered to the three big shots up at midfield. Torry, Marcus, and Javon weren't used to dropping back on defense, since I'd always had things under control. But our defense was as weak as spaghetti without me in the middle. The Alligators kept bringing four guys up and overloading our zone.

"Get set for a long day," the guy who scored the second goal said, pointing at me. He wore a red headband that matched the color of his jersey.

I kept my mouth shut. We were capable of winning big, and I'd rather we bombard them with goals than get into an argument.

But things needed to turn around fast. Sweat was dripping down my back, partly from running and partly from nervousness.

The rest of the half was fast-paced, but I didn't give up any more goals. I even made a couple of saves. But we didn't score either, so we were looking out of a deep 2–0 hole as we trotted off the field at half time.

"Unacceptable," Javon said. "We're much better than they are."

"So far we aren't," I said.

Coach waved us over. "What's our biggest asset?" he asked.

"We score a lot of goals," Marcus said.

"Yeah, but why?"

Marcus shrugged. "We're fast. We can run all day long."

"Exactly," Coach said. "So we're going to make a few adjustments to take better advantage of that."

He pointed to Torry. "You're moving to midfield. It's not a position we've even used this season. On a small field like this, we only needed forwards and defensemen. But the Alligators are overwhelming us on both ends of the field. So Torry is going to roam."

Coach explained how it would work. Jameer would move up to the front line with Marcus and Javon. Torry would play behind them but be a key part of the offense, giving us four men up front. But he'd also be the middle defender, hustling back every time.

"It'll be a lot of running, but you can handle it," Coach said to Torry. "Don't try to be everywhere, but make the middle of the field your zone—from one goal box all the way to the other."

"He can do it," I said. "You could triple the size of the field and Torry would still cover it."

"I'm counting on that," Coach said.

We had five minutes to rest. I sat next to Connor and asked him what he thought.

"You tried your best," he said. "But some of your players aren't very fast."

"The second half will be different."

"It better be," Connor said. He lifted his drink bottle to me, but I had my own.

"Thanks," I said. "Keep watching. If we're as good as we think we are, we'll find a way to win."

FIVE

Momentum

We huddled up near the center circle before the second-half kickoff.

"Listen," Torry said, "I've seen this before." He looked stern and determined. "A team gets a few wins and thinks they're unbeatable. We should've learned last week that we aren't. This second half needs to be more than a comeback. We need to dominate the action. And win!"

When Torry gets on a mission like that, he's hard to stop. So it was no surprise when he scored less than a minute into the half. We were right back in it. Now, could we play defense?

I looked at Charlie, then at Luis.

"No breakaways," I told them. "Don't hang back if the Alligators come charging." They were the only protection I had at the moment. Torry was up front, battling for the ball.

But when the Alligators moved into our end of the field, Torry came with them. Javon and Marcus drifted back, too, so our defense was more solid than before. A weak shot dribbled toward me from way out. I easily picked it up.

I kicked the ball and let out my breath. I hadn't realized I'd been holding it.

Relax, I told myself. *You're ready for this.*

We seemed to have figured out a better system. Maybe those first four games had been too easy—lots of scoring by us and very few chances by our opponents. So we weren't ready for a good team like the Alligators. Fortunately, we had plenty of time left.

Our offense was working better now. Having Jameer up there added an option.

"Don't get greedy!" I yelled when Javon tried too hard to drive to the goal. He was quickly trapped by two Alligators. Marcus was open to Javon's left and Jameer to the right, but it was too late. Javon lost the ball.

The Alligators made a long pass and their tall wing burst past the center line. Torry chased him down, but not until he was deep into our end of the field. Luis ran toward the action, leaving the area in front of the goal wide open.

I took a step forward, keeping between the ball and the goal, and raised my hands. Charlie moved to my left, but three Alligators joined him in the box.

"Where are you guys?" I called. Javon and Marcus needed to get back here, too.

Torry got his foot on the ball and knocked it out-of-bounds.

"Corner kick!" called the referee.

It was the first corner kick I'd faced since that disaster last week. Marcus and Javon ran up. I hugged close to the goalpost, eyes wide.

Just like last week, the ball floated high into the goal box, but this time it didn't hit the ground. Torry jumped higher than anyone and headed the ball off to the side. Javon sent it way up the field. An Alligator defender booted it right back.

Their passes were quick and sharp, moving the ball from player to player like a pinball machine. The red-headband guy broke into the clear.

Here it comes, I thought. Giving up a third goal would be a heartbreaker at this point. I didn't think we could recover from that.

Bwock! The ball curved toward the upper corner of the goal, moving fast. I leaped, managing to get both hands on it. The ball fell to the ground and I jumped on it, hugging it tight. Save!

"Yeah, Griffin!" Torry yelled.

I stood and calmly looked up the field. Jameer was waiting to my left, so I rolled the ball to him.

That save felt like a momentum shifter. The Alligators had taken their best shot. Our turn now.

I glanced toward the sideline. Connor was jumping up and down with his arms raised. "Great catch!" he called.

I gave him a thumbs-up.

My save was the spark we needed. Seconds later, Torry scored again.

Tying the score seemed to deflate the Alligators. We dominated the rest of the game, and I only had to make one more save. Marcus scored to give us the lead, and Javon added the icing on the cake to make it 4–2.

Connor ran onto the field at the final whistle, smacking hands with Torry and the others. Then he rushed to me and gave me a hug. "Great game," he said. "I want to be a goalie!"

I laughed. "I thought you'd want to score goals."

"I'll do that, too," he said. "I'll just run back and forth all game."

We shook hands with the Alligators. They all looked as down as I'd felt the week before. "Long day," I said when I reached the guy with the

headband, rubbing it in a little. He'd beaten me for that second goal, but I'd made two good saves on his other shots.

He sneered.

"Cheer up," I told him.

"Easy for you to say," he mumbled.

I shrugged. "You guys were tough," I said. "It could have gone either way."

I wondered how I'd feel if things had tipped in their favor. Not good. I'd be wishing I'd never become goalie. What if I hadn't made that key save and we'd fallen two goals behind again? Funny how a small change can make such a difference.

As usual, I was plenty hungry after the game. "Stampeder discount at the café," I told my friends.

"Sounds awesome," Torry said. Marcus and Javon agreed, so we headed to Main Street.

We grabbed the last table in the corner.

The waitress smiled at me. She knew that Connor and I would eat for free, of course.

"The special today is turkey with gravy and mashed potatoes," she said. "Sound good?"

"Five of those, please," I said. "And a pitcher of iced tea." I didn't give the others a chance to order anything else. I knew enough about the business to see that the special was a good deal. It was also a better deal for my parents, since my friends had a standing discount when they were with me.

"Whose house are we playing basketball at this afternoon?" Connor asked.

"We had a better idea for today," Javon said. "There's a new movie we want to see. Space aliens try to take over the world. Lots of cool laser battles and stuff."

"Can't you go tonight?" I asked.

Javon shook his head. "It's three bucks cheaper in the afternoon."

That movie would be too scary for Connor. I could drop him off at Julie's, or even let him stay at the café until closing. But neither of those things would be any fun for him. I decided to skip the movie and hang out with my brother.

"We'll play some one-on-one," I told Connor. He looked disappointed, but I couldn't expect my friends to change their plans.

"We'll play hoops tomorrow," Torry said. "Three-on-two again." He held up his palm and Connor smacked it with his own.

We gobbled up the food. Even Torry was tired, since he'd done twice as much running as usual.

The waitress brought three bills.

"Don't forget to tip," I said. I put a dollar on the table, which wasn't much but it was all I had.

Javon borrowed a dollar from Torry. "I'll stop home before the movie," he said. "That meal wiped out my allowance. I'll ask Dad for an advance."

"We'd better hurry," Torry said. "The movie starts in twenty minutes."

They rushed off. I tapped my fingers on the table. "Want dessert?" I asked Connor. I knew he'd been counting on basketball with my friends. But he'd already had a lot more fun than usual for a Saturday morning, so he shouldn't be too disappointed.

Most of the lunch crowd had cleared out of the café. We went into the kitchen.

"There's my boys!" Mom said. "How did your brother do today, Connor?"

"Bad, then good, then great!"

Mom laughed and looked at me. "So I guess you won?"

I nodded. "Yeah. Rough start, but that's how it goes in sports."

"Wish I could have been there," Mom said.

Dad came out of the storeroom with a box. He picked up Connor and growled in his face. "Want to help?" he asked. "I have to refill the salt shakers."

"Don't we get dessert first?" Connor asked.

"Dessert second," Dad said, smiling. "Work first."

They went out to the dining room, so I was alone with Mom in the kitchen.

"I'm so glad you've been spending more time with Connor," she said. "Running this café is a big job, so it's a huge help when you take him."

Mom had been a cook at another restaurant before we moved here, and Dad worked at a bank. But they'd always dreamed of running their own place. When this café became available, they decided to take the chance. I understood, but Connor didn't like being with a sitter so often.

I thought again about the movie. I really wanted to see it, and I could still get to the theater on time. Connor would be fine here for a couple of hours.

Aliens and laser battles, or one-on-one with Connor? I knew which one I'd prefer. A month ago I wouldn't have thought twice. But this wasn't a hard decision. I'd be staying with Connor.

I've been on winning teams before, but my contributions to the success usually weren't big. I was a backup forward on the school basketball team, only getting on the floor for the last few minutes if a game wasn't close. If it was close, I didn't play at all.

I was pretty good in baseball. But most of my teams had been weak.

So this soccer season was different. Obviously I wasn't a scoring machine like Torry, but I was a crucial player.

So I was proud that we were undefeated, and even prouder that I'd overcome my worries about playing goalie. This was the first sports season where I felt like my efforts really mattered.

At home, I tossed the basketball to Connor, but then I had a better idea. I picked up a soccer ball.

"Still want to be a goalie?" I asked.

"Yes!"

"Okay. The garage door is the goal. Try to stop my shots."

Connor stood in front of the garage and clapped his hands. I kicked the ball to his left and it bounced off the door.

"Goal!" I said.

"Wait! I don't have goalie gloves."

"That wouldn't have mattered. You didn't touch the ball."

Connor hurried into the house. He came back a minute later with red winter gloves.

"They'll do," I said. I made a soft kick a little closer to him. He batted it away.

"Nice save," I said. I dribbled around, made a few moves, then kicked. He caught it.

"Let me score now," he said.

"You can try," I said. "I'm pretty good, though."

Connor lined up the ball about fifteen feet from me. His first kick flew over the garage and landed in a neighbor's yard.

"You hit it too low," I said. I demonstrated how a kick in the middle of the ball sent it on a line drive, and how kicking it below the center would pop it into the air.

It didn't take him long to get it right. And stopping his shots was good practice for me. Connor kicked hard for a little guy, and he managed to slip a few past me.

I was ready to stop after a half hour, but he wanted to keep going. "Break time," I said. "You're turning into Torry!"

"What do you mean?" He dribbled the ball with his hand, as if it were a basketball, then took a jump shot that bonked off the rim.

"He goes nonstop, too," I said. "All sports, all the time."

"That's for me!"

"Ha!" I sat on the back steps and watched him shoot baskets.

"We never did get dessert," Connor said after a while. "I was so busy helping Dad that I forgot."

"Let's see what we have," I said. I found a box of cookies in a cabinet and we sat on the couch to

watch TV. We both yawned. Before I knew it, we were both asleep. We didn't wake up until Mom and Dad came home.

"Naps?" Mom said when she found us. "You two haven't napped in years!"

"He wore me out," I said. "That and the game."

"How long did you sleep?"

I yawned again. "Must have been an hour."

"Well, maybe we'll all stay up late for a change," Dad said. "I'm sure we'll still wake up at four thirty, but at least we won't have to run into work." The café is closed on Sundays.

"Let's rent a movie," Mom said. "You can choose, Griffin, since you passed up the one earlier."

"I didn't want to see it anyway," I said, even though I did. "We had a lot of fun, right, Connor?"

"Griffin taught me a lot. He said I'm going to be like Torry."

"Don't you want to be like Griffin?" Mom asked.

"I do! But I want to score goals like his friends."

I stood and stretched. Mom backed away. "You smell kind of gamy," she said. "Better hit the shower." I was still in my soccer clothes.

"Dad and I are going for a walk," Mom said. "We'll grab Thai food. I've been cooking nonstop since six this morning. I don't even want to look at a stove!"

I decided to check the league standings on the YMCA site before I got cleaned up. We were still on top, but the Lawnmowers had me concerned.

	W	L	T:
Stampeders	5	0	1
Lawnmowers	4	1	1
Cyclones	3	2	1
Onions	3	3	1
Moose	3	3	0
Alligators	2	3	1
Sharks	2	3	1
Armadillos	2	4	0
Skateboards	0	5	2

Today's scores:
Armadillos 3, Skateboards 2
Lawnmowers 6, Sharks 0
Stampeders 4, Alligators 2
Cyclones 5, Moose 4

Next Saturday's games:
Lawnmowers vs. Armadillos, 9 a.m.
Stampeders vs. Skateboards, 10:15 a.m.
Cyclones vs. Alligators, 11:30 a.m.
Moose vs. Sharks, 12:45 p.m.

Final week:
Onions vs. Cyclones, 9 a.m.
Moose vs. Alligators, 10:15 a.m.
Sharks vs. Armadillos, 11:30 a.m.
Stampeders vs. Lawnmowers, 12:45 p.m.

By the way, we made up our own team names at the first practice session. I suggested Polar Bears, but everybody else voted for Stampeders. Mine wouldn't have counted anyway, since we later learned that only one-word names were acceptable. That's how the Mighty Fighting Roaring Eagles turned into the Onions.

We'd get another good look at the Lawnmowers right before our next game. Assuming we both won, then the league title would be decided when we played them in the final game of the season.

One thing was certain: we controlled our own destiny. The Skateboards hadn't won a game all season, so we'd trounce them next week. As long as we took care of business against the Lawnmowers, we'd be the champs.

SEVEN
Big Mouth

On Monday, our algebra teacher had us team up to solve some problems, so I took a seat next to Spencer. He had a smaller wrap on his wrist, but he couldn't write very well yet. His T-shirt said MEMORIAL DAY TRIATHLON.

"Looks like an easy game coming up," he said. "I scouted the Skateboards, and they're not very skilled."

"Maybe I can switch out of playing goalie when we build a big lead," I said. "It'd be nice to have a chance to score a goal."

Spencer nodded. "The goalie's dream. Wish I could get on the field again, but my parents would never let me."

"Neither would Coach," I said.

"Next year."

"Griffin?" the teacher asked.

"Yes?"

"Have you solved the problems yet?"

I blushed. "Not quite."

"Work on soccer after school, please."

I blushed, and we went back to algebra. But our teacher was cool. I knew suddenly we'd see soccer-themed word problems showing up on a test.

Tuesday's practice went well and so did Thursday's. We worked on transitions—pushing the ball forward on offense and hustling back when our opponent had the ball. Torry was the key to it all, but Coach had Marcus take some turns as the midfielder, just in case.

Of course, you can't really practice game situations with only eight players. So we ran

through the strategy a few times on Thursday, then went into a four-on-four scrimmage.

"No goalies," Coach said. "Spread out and move. I want to see constant passing."

That was hard. A half hour of scrimmaging had me wheezing. But I recovered quickly. It felt good to be on the field again, out of the goal box.

Friday at lunch I waited in the cafeteria line with Javon. I usually make my own lunch to bring, but Friday is pizza day, and we never miss that.

"Did you hear about Jameer?" he asked.

I shook my head. Jameer had been looking a little pale and rundown the day before, but he hadn't complained.

"Strep throat," Javon said. "We won't see him this weekend."

"Better this week than next," I said. With Jameer sidelined, we'd have no substitutes for

Saturday's game, but we weren't expecting much of a challenge anyway. "We'll need him back against the Lawnmowers."

"Yeah." Javon laughed. "We could beat the Skateboards with three guys. We won't miss Jameer at all."

The guy behind Javon cleared his throat and I looked back to see a gray SKATEBOARDS shirt. I nudged Javon.

"Sorry, Davey," Javon said with a big grin. "Just joking around."

"We'll see," Davey said. He didn't smile back. Davey is a pretty good player—short and strong and fast—but the rest of his team isn't so good. You can't win a soccer game by yourself, which is why they hadn't won at all.

"Javon didn't mean anything," I said to Davey. "We just found out that another one of our players is out. So Javon was saying, like, we should do okay."

"Sure," Davey said. "I heard the whole thing."

"I was just saying we're lucky to be playing you this week instead of the Lawnmowers," Javon said. That didn't make it any better.

"Shut your big mouth," I whispered.

Davey pushed past us and headed for a table. "See you tomorrow," he said. "On the field."

I elbowed Javon, and he juggled his tray. "Nice going," I said. "Getting them all stirred up."

"Just one guy."

"Like he won't tell everybody on his team?" I said.

"Who cares? We'll beat them by ten goals."

"Probably," I said. The Skateboards would be playing their last game of the season. Since there were nine teams in the league, one was off every week. It was their turn. We'd had our week off a month ago. With a big zero in the win column, the Skateboards would be extra psyched to break through. Nobody wants a winless season.

"You never want to give an opponent extra incentive," I said.

"Incentive won't help them," Javon said. "I'm not worried at all."

I wasn't either. But I didn't like being a poor sport or a show-off.

Friday night my family plays board games together. We try to do it every Friday, but it usually works out to two or three times a month.

We stick to easy games until Connor starts falling asleep, then switch to Monopoly or Scrabble. It feels old-fashioned to be playing board games and leaving the computer off, but that's just how my parents are.

"This game has an online version," I said.

"I'm sure it does," Dad said. "We could all go to our own closets and play against the computer. Ah, family bonding."

"We should go all out and play by candlelight," I joked, rolling the dice. "Pretend electricity never even happened."

"We're not *that* retro," Mom said. "Besides, I just bought Electric Company." She held up one of the Monopoly cards. "And you owe me thirty-two dollars."

I handed over the fake money. "I was totally kidding about the online version," I said.

Playing games with my parents was calming. I felt grown-up when we talked about things like the restaurant business or school. It wasn't like the video games I played with Torry and the others, when we were trashing each other and joking around the whole time.

Dad landed on one of my cheap properties and handed me six dollars. "Robbery!" he said with a smile.

I yawned and stretched. "Early start tomorrow," I said. "Have to be there for the nine o'clock game."

"Connor will have you up by six," Mom said. "He's so excited that you're taking him again."

"Me too. I think I'll drop out of this one. Maybe we can pick it up tomorrow night?"

"Fine by me," Dad said.

I went to my room and listened to some music, lying on my bed in the dark. I was tired, but I was excited about the game. I imagined myself making some tough, diving saves, but I probably wouldn't have to do that. First-place team vs. last-place team. Should be an easy win. We hadn't had one of those in a while. The past two games had been hard.

I sat up. I don't know why, but I put on the goalie gloves. They felt right. I belonged in them. As much as I'd resisted becoming the goalie, it seemed like I'd found my place.

For this season, at least.

Our entire team (except Jameer) showed up at the field before nine o'clock on Saturday, eager to watch the Lawnmowers take on the Armadillos. Connor brought a poster that said GO STAMPEDERS with little soccer players he'd drawn.

The Lawnmowers needed a win to make certain that next week's game would be for the title. We already had five wins, and they had four.

The possibilities looked like this: After we beat the Skateboards, our record would be 6 wins, 0 losses, 1 tie. With a win today, the Lawnmowers would be 5–1–1. If they happened to lose (not very likely), we'd clinch the championship. A tie would push them to 4–1–2, and we'd still be champs because they couldn't get to six wins.

We expected them to win though. Then, if they beat us next week, we'd both have the same record (6–1–1). They'd win the championship because they beat us head-to-head.

But that was not going to happen. We were confident we'd beat them, even if we'd already clinched the title. We wanted to go undefeated.

We had lots of soccer ahead before any of that would matter.

The Lawnmowers took an early lead over the Armadillos and stretched it to 2–0 by half time. We jogged to one of the smaller fields to warm up.

We were ready for anything today. Our passes were crisp, and everybody had a ton of confidence. The morning was cool and there was no humidity, so it felt like we could run all day. Even without any substitutes, our energy should last.

I was passing the ball back and forth with Marcus when Spencer ran over from the main field.

"You guys should come see this!" he called.

"What's up?" I asked.

"The Armadillos just tied the score."

"No way!" That was unexpected, but it could be great news for us. We all hurried to watch the end of the game.

The Lawnmowers attacked the goal, firing shot after shot. But the Armadillos goalie stopped every one.

When the final whistle blew, the Lawnmowers walked off, looking glum. The Armadillos celebrated as if they'd won the championship.

Coach called us over. "We're next," he said. "Play smart. You just saw what can happen. Even a strong team can be surprised by a weaker one."

"Not us," Javon said, shooting off his big mouth again. "The Armadillos just gave us the title."

Torry laughed. "Give us the trophies!"

Coach shook his head. "Not yet, guys. You still have to win today."

Ramon replaced Jameer as our third forward for this game, so Charlie and Luis were my defenders. I didn't expect they'd have to do too much, and the beginning of the game proved that.

Torry led the way as we dominated the opening minutes. The Skateboards goalie was good, and he managed two saves. But we kept the pressure on, and the ball never left their end of the field.

Marcus got off a rocket of a kick, and Torry, Javon, and Ramon charged after it in case there was a rebound. The ball smacked the crossbar and bounced way up the field. Suddenly Davey had the ball near midfield, with our players way behind him. A second Skateboard was trailing Davey.

"Stop them!" I called to Charlie and Luis.

Both defenders ran toward the ball. The second Skateboard looped around them as Davey kicked the ball forward. Luis and Charlie ran to the ball, but the Skateboard got there first. He made a soft pass back to Davey, who was wide open.

It was just me and him. One-on-one. He was running right up the middle of the field, so I couldn't do much about the angle. A shot to either corner would be tough to get to.

He faked left, then right, still coming at me full speed. I spread my arms wide. He shot.

The ball spun past me, into the goal.

Davey leaped with his fist in the air.

Javon had sprinted the length of the field, but he arrived too late. He dropped to his knees and shook his head. "Lucky play," he said. "Wouldn't happen again in a million years."

"No big deal," I said softly. "We'll get it right back and then some." If Marcus's shot had been a couple of inches lower, then we'd have a 1–0 lead, not them.

I picked up the ball and rolled it toward the center circle.

Connor held up his sign. I smiled. Clapped my hands. "Let's go!" I called.

My teammates weren't thrown off by the goal. We were back on the attack in seconds, and Javon nearly headed one into the net before the goalie batted it away. Then Torry's corner kick caused chaos in front of the goal, but Davey managed to kick it out-of-bounds.

"Settle down!" I yelled. We should have had two or three goals by now. But the Skateboards were packing their entire team into the defensive zone, so it was hard for us to get a clear shot.

Ramon kicked one that looked perfect, but at the last second it curved and nicked the goalpost. The goalie fell on it. Another near miss.

Late in the half, the Skateboards crossed midfield for only the second time all game. They patiently passed the ball, keeping it just out of our reach and inching forward.

I bounced on my toes. The game was fun to watch, but I really hadn't done anything yet. A little more action would be good.

Davey brought the ball to the corner, with Charlie blocking his path. Torry, Marcus, and Luis had the other Skateboards covered. I crouched by the goalpost, eyes on the ball, ready to spring.

Davey made a quick move and darted past Charlie, heading for the box. I had a perfect angle to block any shot, but he had some open field ahead. Luis raced over to block his way, jutting his foot toward the ball.

Davey went down, falling over Luis's outstretched leg. The ball rolled free and I grabbed it. But the ref blasted his whistle.

"That was a trip," he said. "I'm awarding the Skateboards a penalty kick."

"I didn't do it on purpose," Luis said. "I was just going for the ball."

"It's still a penalty," the ref said. "I know it wasn't intentional, or you'd be out of the game."

He set the ball on the penalty spot, twelve yards out from the goal.

Davey glared at me. I tried to guess where he'd kick it.

Coach had very briefly told me how to defend a penalty kick. There wasn't much to it. You had to make your best estimate of where the shot would go, based on instinct and the shooter's body language.

Davey had scored that first goal by shooting to my right. Would he do that again? Or would he try to fool me by going in the opposite direction?

A goalie has no time to recover if he makes the wrong move on a penalty kick. I shifted back and forth, hoping I could lunge to either side in time.

Davey ran forward. His shot was low, just a few inches off the ground, and headed left. I dove, got a hand on it, and slowed it down. But it kept trickling and I couldn't reach it. It crossed the line for another goal, and suddenly we were 2–0.

It stayed that way until half time. Nobody said a word as we sat on the bench and ate oranges. Everybody was down.

"Come on, guys," Javon finally said. "That's the worst team in the league over there. We're supposed to be the best."

Torry stood up. "We have short memories," he said. "We were down 2–0 at half time last week, too, remember? How'd that end up?"

We all knew the answer. We'd scored four second-half goals.

"Plenty of time," I said.

Javon stared out at the field. "Two cheap goals for them. Two hit posts for us. Our luck has to turn around, right?"

"We have to make our own luck," I said. "Keep pushing. Keep shooting. The balls will find the net. We can't lose this one."

"They're better than I thought they were," Javon said. "Not much offense, but they're tough to score on. Anyway, we're the better team by a long shot. Let's show it!"

I glanced behind me at the small bleachers. Most of the Lawnmowers were up there, looking a lot happier than they did a while ago. They could still win the title if we didn't pull this one out.

I nudged Javon. "Let's ruin their day," I said.

"We'll ruin the Lawnmowers' day, we'll ruin the Skateboards' day, we'll ruin everybody's day," he said.

I laughed. "Except ours."

"Exactly!" he said, and we high-fived.

The Skateboards stayed with their patient strategy in the second half. Their tight defense kept us from getting any breakaways, so we spent a lot of frustrating time passing the ball around and taking less-than-perfect shots.

With a 2–0 lead, Davey and his teammates were content to sit back and preserve the margin. But we couldn't let them wait it out.

All the action was down at the Skateboards' end of the field. Midway through the half, I called to Coach. "Can we send these guys up?"

Coach nodded.

"Go on up, Charlie," I said. "Play offense." I directed Luis to go to the center line, and even I abandoned the goal and went halfway up to the center. I'd have plenty of time to get back if I needed to.

The move worked. Torry played the ball back to Charlie, and he kicked it across to Marcus. A quick pass finally found Torry open, and he scored.

Whew. What a relief. Trimming the lead to a single goal was huge. We could wipe that out with one kick. "Back to normal," I called to Charlie and Luis.

But normal wasn't enough today. The Skateboards killed time with short passes, barely trying to move the ball forward. Our guys were tired. Marcus, Javon, Torry, and Ramon had been running nonstop. The Skateboards had two more players than we did, and their coach had substituted freely. We were running out of gas.

"One minute left," the referee called.

This was our last chance to avoid an embarrassing loss.

"Go," I said to my defenders. They rushed up the field.

Marcus took a shot that the goalie batted away. Javon reached the free ball and shot, but it hit a defender, who booted it up toward midfield. Charlie retreated and brought it back.

I was counting the seconds in my head. Nothing to lose now. I ran up the field.

Charlie was swarmed by a pack of defenders.

"Here!" I called. I fielded his pass and dribbled, then passed to Ramon. He looked for Torry and tried to force the ball his way. But Davey got there first. He took two dribbles and kicked it the length of the field.

I sprinted back and reached the ball deep in the corner. But before I could turn, the ref blew his whistle.

Game over.

Title in jeopardy.

Big mouths shut.

NINE

Regrouping

I was stunned that we lost, but I took a tiny bit of pleasure when Javon had to shake Davey's hand.

"Where were those three guys?" Davey asked.

Javon looked startled. "What three guys?"

"The ones who could beat us all by themselves?"

Javon rolled his eyes. "I was just kidding around." He stuck out his hand. "You shut me up. Nice game, all right?"

Davey shook his hand. "You too." He had a huge grin when he got to me. "Never underestimate us," he said. "We got better every week."

We hadn't. Our past three games had been a struggle, even though we'd only lost one of them. We needed to regroup and focus on next week's showdown with the Lawnmowers. Our "championship" season was on the brink.

"Better keep that poster," I said to Connor as we walked home. "We'll need the inspiration next week."

"I might make a new one," he said. "This one didn't work."

Javon, Torry, and Marcus walked quietly behind us. They almost never went more than a few seconds before cracking a joke or something, but we were halfway home before anyone spoke.

"You never know," Torry said.

That summed it up.

We went to my house and sat on the porch with lemonade. Connor played with his toy trucks in the driveway. Nobody felt like doing much.

"Are we really that bad all of a sudden?" Marcus asked. "I mean, the Skateboards are a lot better than their record says, but come on. They made us look like beginners."

"Let's just forget about it," Torry said. He picked up some dry pine needles and crumpled them between his fingers. "Everything we did today turned out wrong."

"This season started out so great," Javon said. "Four shutouts, on our way to a fifth. Then Spencer went down. That seems like a year ago."

"Hey, it's not because of Spencer," I said. I didn't like him implying that the goalie was the problem.

"That was the turning point," Javon said. "And I'm not saying it's your fault. Our whole style changed. We needed you on defense to keep things rolling. Those other guys didn't get it done."

Torry set down his glass. "They play just as hard as you do," he said. "Team, remember? T-E-A-M. That's how we win, that's how we lose."

I pointed at Javon. "And you didn't help any by getting Davey all riled up."

"That wasn't the only reason they won. And you were there, too," he said sharply.

"Yeah, and I told you to shut up." I finished my lemonade and went into the house to find chips. When I came back, Javon gave me a cold stare.

"Hey, guys," Marcus said. "Chill out. We lost, okay? No reason to be grouches about it."

Javon reached into the bag for some chips. "Wish we could play them again," he mumbled. "Should have been seven-zip today."

"Should have been," Torry said sarcastically. "Wasn't! Let's stop talking about it. Worst game I ever played."

Torry stepped off the porch. "Where's your soccer ball?" he asked.

"I'll get it!" Connor said, running off.

Connor tossed the ball to Torry.

Torry dribbled toward the garage, narrating every move. "Here's Marcus with the ball, wide open! He shoots!" Torry kicked the ball off the garage. "Oooow, off the crossbar. The Stampeders watch it roll toward midfield. They stand still like statues." He ran toward the ball, which had rolled nearly to the street, then dribbled it back up the driveway. "Now Davey has the ball, racing toward Griffin, who's all alone in front of the goal. He shoots. He scores!"

Marcus clapped lightly. "Nice replay," he said.

"That's about how it went," Torry said. "We just watched that guy go end to end with the ball."

"I didn't," Javon said. "I was right behind him."

"We still should've won," Marcus said. "What's one goal? Even two. We should've had eight."

Torry dropped to the porch again and leaned against the house. "Let's just forget about that game," he said again. "That wasn't us."

"Yeah," Marcus said. "We're better than that."

Then we were quiet for several minutes. I don't know what the others were thinking, but I was wondering if we *were* any better.

That night, I checked the league standings. I knew the deal, but seeing it online cemented it in my brain. Win or tie next week and we were champs. A loss would drop us to second. We still controlled our fate.

	W	L	T:
Stampeders	5	1	1
Lawnmowers	4	1	2
Moose	4	3	0
Cyclones	3	3	1
Alligators	3	3	1
Onions	3	3	1
Armadillos	2	4	1
Sharks	2	4	1
Skateboards	1	5	2

Today's scores:
Lawnmowers 2, Armadillos 2
Skateboards 2, Stampeders 1
Alligators 4, Cyclones 3
Moose 3, Sharks 0

Final week:
Onions vs. Cyclones, 9 a.m.
Moose vs. Alligators, 10:15 a.m.
Sharks vs. Armadillos, 11:30 a.m.
Stampeders vs. Lawnmowers, 12:45 p.m.

It rained hard again on Tuesday and never let up, so Coach canceled practice for the first time. That was probably for the best. A little break from soccer might have been all we needed. Thursday's session went very well. We were all business.

On Friday night, Torry's parents invited us over for a "celebration of the soccer season." I reminded everyone that we didn't have anything to celebrate yet.

"It's always worth celebrating a hard-fought season," Mrs. Santana replied. They had a cake and hot dogs.

Most of the team showed up, but we tried not to talk about soccer. We all knew what we had to do. And what we couldn't let happen again.

I got into a four-man Ping-Pong game. Marcus and me against Javon and Spencer. Spencer had to play left-handed, but he wasn't bad. As usual, it

got super competitive. That's just how things go with these guys.

We won.

"Rematch," Javon said. "We barely got warmed up for that one."

"Just one more," I said.

"Two out of three."

"Like I said," I replied with a smirk, serving the ball. "One more."

We won that one, too. I went to get a piece of cake. Javon called Torry over to take my place.

"They go nonstop, don't they?" Torry's dad said to me as he sat down with his cake.

"Mm-hmm," I said, my mouth full of chocolate frosting. "It pays off in sports. Gets a little old off the field sometimes."

Mr. Santana laughed. "I'm looking forward to tomorrow," he said. "Missed the past few games."

"It's good that you get to some," I said. "My parents can't. They come to my summer baseball games 'cause those are in the evenings. But there's no way they could leave the café on a Saturday morning."

That didn't bother me. Sure, it would be nice to have my whole family at a game, but I knew the score. They were doing their best for me and Connor.

"Yes!" Javon yelled. We all looked over to the Ping-Pong table. Javon and Spencer had managed to beat Marcus and Torry.

"Rematch!" Torry said.

Where had I heard that before?

At least their minds were off soccer for a few minutes. Mine was going right back to it. I wanted this championship.

It was right there for the taking.

Connor was in my room at five thirty the next morning, already wearing the STAMPEDERS shirt. He poked my arm and bugged me to get up. He held up his new poster:

STAMPEDE THE LAWNMOWERS!!!!

"That's good," I said. "Did Mom help you with the spelling?"

"A little."

I brought one hand out from under the covers and held out my palm. He slapped it.

"The game isn't until noon," I said. "You've got a long wait."

"Can we go to the field and watch the other games?"

"Just the one before ours," I said. "I don't want to be out in the sun all morning. It zaps my energy. Besides, the first game doesn't start for three and a half hours."

"Maybe we can play basketball."

"Another energy zapper," I said. "Tell you what we can do though. We can walk to the café and have breakfast. That'll be a nice surprise for Mom and Dad."

The morning was cold, and the sun wasn't even up yet when we left the house. The streets were mostly empty, but the café was already buzzing with customers when we arrived. We went straight to the kitchen.

"Surprise!" Connor said.

"Did you eat your cereal?" Mom asked.

"No. We want to eat here!"

Mom laughed. "I have a few orders ahead of you, but give me a few minutes." She winked at me, and we went to grab boxes to sit on.

We devoured Mom's best pancakes and ham.

"Good luck," she said when we left.

"Thanks," I said. I hoped we wouldn't need it.

We went home and watched TV for the rest of the morning.

It was much warmer by the time we got to the field. Torry and Marcus were sitting in the bleachers. Connor ran over to them. I stayed on the sideline to study the goalies. After a while, Spencer tapped me on the shoulder.

"The doctor said I could play."

"Get out!"

"I'm serious." He held up his wrist. It had been bare at the party. Now it was lightly taped. "Not goalie. But I can play a little D if I'm careful."

"Does Coach know?"

"Yeah. I called him this morning."

That was good news. Jameer was getting better, but he wasn't really ready to play. So having Spencer as a sub was crucial.

"I wasn't going to, but last night everybody was talking about winning the championship," Spencer said. "The doctor cleared me to play earlier in the week, but I didn't tell anybody. I wasn't sure if I wanted to or not."

"Why not?"

"I thought I might be too tentative, you know? Holding back because I'd be worried about reinjuring this. But the more we talked last night, the more I wanted to play. So, here I am."

I could see the Lawnmowers on the other field, already warming up in their blue jerseys. I did a few jumping jacks.

"I'd better get a ball," Spencer said. "I'm out of practice."

We found one under the bleachers. I called Connor over, and the three of us passed it back and forth.

At game time, we gathered around Coach. "We're playing to win," he said. "We all know a tie would be enough to win the championship, but we're not interested in a tie. Let's finish this season the way we started it, with a dominating victory."

"Let's go!" we shouted.

My teammates ran onto the field. I walked. I wasn't being lazy, I just wanted to drink it all in. There weren't a lot of spectators, but I didn't care. This was important. I savored it.

I knew a few of the Lawnmowers from school. Their big scorers were Diego and Ryan. Their goalie was good, too.

Diego took the kickoff, and they came right at us. The game was going to be nonstop, I could tell.

"Stay in tight," I told Charlie and Luis. All of our frontline guys rushed back to help on D.

I spread my fingers. *Just try to get it past me.*

My first test came within seconds. Luis knocked down a crossing pass and booted it hard, but Ryan got a foot on the ball and slid it to Diego.

His shot was high but just below the crossbar. I jumped, punching it into the air. It came down directly in front of me. Torry kicked fast to get it out of our goal, but it went out-of-bounds behind the goal.

The corner kick resulted in another hard shot, which Marcus deflected away. But the flurry continued. I caught a line drive from Ryan. Lawnmower attack averted!

"Great work!" Spencer called from the bench. I heard Connor yelling for me too.

I drop-kicked the ball way up the field. My confidence was soaring now. I could stop anything they kicked at me.

"Ohhhh!" Charlie said as Torry's shot went just wide on the other end of the field. "That looked good."

The Lawnmowers' style was a lot like ours—constant attacking. Nothing like our previous game, where the opponent was cautious on offense and very committed to defense. It looked like we were in for a frantic back-and-forth game.

A game where a great goalie could make all the difference.

"Here they come again," I said.

Charlie and Luis were already on it. Luis raced to the ball and Charlie moved toward Ryan. The Lawnmowers found seams in our defense and kept making precision passes. Diego shot again from close range.

Another save!

This is like a basketball game, I thought as my teammates made another charge toward the Lawnmowers' goal. No one had scored yet, but both teams had had chances.

I'd made five saves by the midpoint of the half, and two other shots had gone wide. Ryan finally teed off from the top of the goal box, sending a spinning shot out of my reach. The Lawnmowers had the lead.

"No problem," Torry said. "We've been behind before."

Yeah. Twice. And last week we never came back. But I knew this game would be different. We were getting plenty of chances, too.

Spencer came in to sub for Luis. He bumped my fist, left-handed, and took his position.

"I'm nervous," he said.

"That'll go away as soon as you touch the ball," I said. That was always the case in sports. You get keyed up and worried before a game, but once the action starts you forget that.

Spencer didn't wait long. Diego stole the ball from Javon and sprinted along the sideline. Spencer knocked the ball out-of-bounds. Diego scooped it up and made a deep throw-in, finding a teammate straight out from the goal. He turned and shot, and I made my sixth save.

With three Lawnmowers by our goal, I kicked the ball as far as I could. It soared past the center line, and Torry chased it down. We finally had a mismatch, with three others up there and only two defenders.

Torry kicked the ball to Marcus, who darted ahead, then passed to Ramon as a defender met him at the top of the box. Ramon lunged right, drawing the goalie to that side, then crossed the ball to Torry for the tying goal.

"There we go!" I shouted.

At half time, Javon plopped onto the bench and drank an entire bottle of water in one motion. "That pace is insane," he said.

"I love it," Torry said. "That's our kind of game. The Lawnmowers are tired. I can tell."

Javon laughed. "And we aren't?"

"Not me," Torry said. He hadn't even sat down. "I'm ready for more." Then he pointed toward the parking lot and grinned until I looked that way.

My parents were running toward us. Dad raised his arms when he spotted me.

“Who’s covering the café?” I called over to them.

“We closed early!” Mom said with a laugh. “Didn’t even clear the dishes from the tables.”

“Wow!” I said. That meant a lot to me. “I’ll go back with you after the game. Connor and I will help you clean up.”

“I’ll do the dishes!” Connor said. He loved getting soaked at the giant sink.

Now I really had to play well. But having my parents at the game didn’t feel like pressure. It gave me confidence.

The second half started as wildly as the first, but as the minutes ticked away, everyone started to slow down. A tie would work for us. We’d be champs. But a win would be sweeter.

Late in the game, Diego crossed midfield with the ball, dodging past Ramon. Spencer ran toward him, forcing him to the sideline, but Diego kept control and came deep into our end.

"Stay with him!" I yelled. Spencer got a foot on the ball and knocked it free. It rolled over the end line, setting up a corner kick.

All of our players ran back and packed into the goal box. Diego floated the ball. I tensed, hands up. A Lawnmower headed the ball sharply.

Out of my reach.

"Goal!" The Lawnmowers had the lead.

No. It can't end this way.

"How much time?" I asked as I tossed the ball to the ref.

"Just over two minutes," he said.

"Go up," I said to Spencer. "We need to score in a hurry."

With five offensive players, we made another big charge. There was always the chance that the Lawnmowers would get a breakaway, but we had to risk it.

Torry kept the ball alive, pivoting and charging. But we couldn't find an opening. Marcus finally broke through the traffic and took a hard shot, but the goalie deflected it away.

Corner kick.

I don't know what got into me. I sprinted up the field. "Stay back," I said to Luis as I passed by.

Marcus had the ball in the corner. Every player was close to the goal. I kept running.

"Here!" I yelled.

Instead of popping the ball into the air in front of the goal, Marcus slid it toward me. No one was within fifteen yards, so I took three dribbles. That drew two defenders toward me, opening up the box. At the last second I nudged the ball past the defenders to Torry. He stopped it with his foot, turned, and fired.

Whoosh! The ball rippled the back of the net. I raised both arms. Marcus grabbed me in a bear hug. "Great play," he whispered. "Brilliant."

My parents were whooping and clapping.

"Defense!" Coach shouted.

I ran back to the goal. Caught my breath.

The seconds ticked away.

The ref blew his whistle. We were the champions!

"We did it!" Javon yelled, whacking me on the shoulder. He was right. The final score was 2—2, but a tie still felt like a huge win.

Connor threw his arms around me.

Best game I'd ever played, in any sport.

Sweetest "win" ever.